D0541598

JN 03469248

Mr Skip

★ MICHAEL
MORPURGO

ILLUSTRATED BY GRIFF

ROARING GOOD READS

Collins

An imprint of HarperCollinsPublishers

For
Léa, Eloise, Alice, Lucie
and
Clare,
because you all love Barnaby so much.

First published in Great Britain by Collins in 2002
Collins is an imprint of HarperCollins*Publishers* Ltd
77-85 Fulham Palace Road, Hammersmith, London W6 8JB

The HarperCollins website address is www.**fire**and**water**.com

1 3 5 7 9 8 6 4 2

Text copyright © Michael Morpurgo 2002
Illustrations by Griff 2002

ISBN 0 00 713474 6

The author asserts the moral right to be
identified as the author of the work.

Printed and bound in England by
Clays Ltd, St Ives plc

CHAPTER ONE

In which I find Mister Skip

I was forever finding things in that rusty old yellow skip. It was on the corner of the estate by the phone box. Whenever they wanted to get rid of stuff, people from all around used to come and dump things in our skip. I'd go have a look and a good mooch around in there whenever I felt like it.

At first Mum told me I shouldn't do it because there might be something in the skip that could cut me or prick me or whatever. So I promised her I'd be careful, and after that she was always fine about it. What made her really happy though was when I brought things home. We didn't have much in our flat – we couldn't afford to buy much at all – so quite a lot of what we did have came out of that rusty old skip.

I found the blue china horse for the mantelpiece, and Mum was thrilled to bits with it, even though it had a chipped nose and only three and a half legs. Her favourite armchair came off the skip too, as well as the electric radiator. All we had to get was a plug for that and it worked perfectly. But best of all was the twenty-six inch Sony Trinitron television set that I brought home in a wheelbarrow – my cousin Barry gave me a hand. It worked fine except that one of the knobs was missing and the colour was a bit fuzzy. Mum didn't mind. She was over the moon about it.

Mum often told me I was "a terrible little jackdaw". And each time she said it she thought it was really funny, because my name is Jackie Dawson, which sounds a bit like jackdaw – if you see what I'm saying. It's not exactly hilarious, is it? But Mum thinks it is. Mum loves a laugh, but there's one thing she takes very seriously indeed. Mum likes to keep up appearances. She doesn't like other people looking down on us or laughing at us – nor do I come to that – which is why she never liked the idea of the neighbours seeing a child of hers crawling about on the skip after other people's cast-offs. That was why I only ever went rummaging around the skip at dusk or after dark.

I don't like to upset Mum, because there's
just the two of us, and as she says, we make
a great team – her and me against the world.
And our world is the estate. There's things I
like about it – I mean, all my friends live here –
but there's lots I don't like about it. It's a grey
place, and you can't see the sky because
there's tower blocks everywhere, and some
people are sad all the time and don't smile.
We haven't got much to do on our estate,

except watch TV. So most evenings in summer we have races, horse races, and then there's the big race on Saturday afternoons. I reckon we've got more horses around our place than on any other estate in the whole wide world. They're tough little horses too. They've got to be. They live out all the year round, in all weathers, and they soon eat down all the grass, so they've never got much to eat. Some people don't look after their horses as well as

they should either and I don't like that. I always thought that if I ever got rich, I would build a stable for every horse on the estate.

Most of the boys on the estate have horses, and a few of the girls too; but the girls aren't allowed to race. It's a boys only thing. The boys call themselves the Crazy Cossacks, and they don't allow the girls to join in even if they do have horses. If you haven't got a

horse on this estate, then you're a no-one. If you're a girl and you haven't got a horse, like me, then you're a no-one twice over. All I've got is that three and a half legged blue china one on the mantelpiece. The one thing I've always longed for all my life is a real live horse of my own that I could look after, that would go as fast as the wind, faster than any of the Crazy Cossacks' horses.

For just a few weeks last year I was allowed to ride on Dasher, Barry's horse. Barry's a little less horrible than most of the other boys on the estate. He's certainly a lot less horrible than Marty Morgan, but then there's no-one as horrible as Marty Morgan.

Marty's the chief of the Crazy Cossacks, and he's a great big oaf, all loud and lumpy, and everyone's frightened of him, except me. I'm *terrified* of him, so *I* keep well out of his way. Even Barry, who's as big as he is, won't stand up to him.

Barry's alright when he's alone with me. When his friends aren't watching he can be really quite nice. I'd been begging him for years to let me have a go on Dasher. All Barry would ever let me do was groom him, or feed him or pick out his hooves – and he wouldn't let me do that very often. Then last year when he got glandular fever, he let me ride him out – not in the races mind – just to exercise him for when Barry got better – which he did, and a bit too soon for my liking. But meanwhile I rode Dasher every moment I could. I had the best time of my life. All I'd ever ridden before was Barnaby, Gran's old donkey who's about as old and slow as Gran is. So to ride Dasher for a while was a real treat, even if I couldn't join in the races round the estate with the Crazy Cossacks.

Anyway, late one evening last week, I was out watching the races, watching Marty Morgan and Barry and the rest of the other Crazy Cossacks as they thundered past me whooping and yelling like a bunch of idiots.

I was feeling all miserable and angry. I so wanted to be out there with them, racing them, beating them. To be honest, I was secretly hoping that Barry would fall off, and break his collar bone or something, so that I could ride Dasher again instead of him. Then I noticed a car backing up to the skip. A man got out, opened up the boot of his car, lifted something out and chucked it into the skip. I remember wondering what it was and thinking I'd find out later. Then I forgot all about it for a while, because suddenly Barry *did* fall off. Sadly for me he didn't break anything.

After that I was busy for a while catching Dasher. It was always really dangerous for a horse if he was running loose on the estate. They were safe enough in their crowded little paddock behind the estate where most of them lived, or even when they were hobbled and grazing on the grass around the flats; but if they broke free and ran off, then they could be straight out onto the open road and in amongst the cars. We'd had a lot of horses knocked over like that, and I wasn't going to let it happen to Dasher.

He was in a bit of a panic, so it took me a while to sweeten him in, catch him and calm him down. Barry thanked me as he mounted up again, and said I could groom Dasher tomorrow if I liked. Big deal, I thought. But I didn't dare say anything. If I upset Barry too much he wouldn't even let me do that. One day Barry, I thought, one day I'm going to ride in the races myself and I'll leave you standing, you and your stupid Crazy Cossacks. I'll beat the lot of you, you see if I don't.

As I made my way home later in the

gathering dusk I was still angry, still dreaming of having my very own horse, and talking to myself out loud as I often did. "There won't be another like him," I was saying. "He'll be the fastest on the estate, the fastest in all Ireland, the fastest in the world. And I'll be riding into the winner's enclosure at the Irish Derby, and I'll leap out of my stirrups like Frankie Dettori. I'll be the greatest."

I was still talking to myself as I came past the skip. That was when I remembered about the car backing up, and that man chucking something in. I thought I might as well have a look. I made sure there was no-one about, then hoisted myself up and into the skip. I couldn't see all that well, and at first there didn't seem to be much that was new. In fact it was almost empty.

Then I saw him. He was lying there on an

old mattress at the bottom of the skip, and he was looking up at me. Well his head was, his face was, but the top part of him was separated from the rest. The other half of him, a very round pot belly and stubby little legs with pointed boots on the end of them, and the toadstool he was sitting on, lay inside a discarded pushchair. In my mind I put the two halves of him together, and recognised him for what he was – a gnome, a battered old garden gnome.

I felt suddenly very sad, very sorry for him, lying there all broken and abandoned and unloved in the bottom of a dirty old skip. I couldn't leave him there like that. I just couldn't. And then I had this totally brilliant idea. I'd fix him up, I'd give him to Mum for her birthday in a fortnight's time. She'd love him, she'd love him to bits.

So, crouching over him and picking up his head I told him my plan. "I'm going to save you," I said. The moonlight fell on his face, and I could see he was a happy smiling sort of gnome. I thought of his name just like that.

"Mister Skip. I'm going to call you Mister Skip, and you'll be coming home with me. I'll put you together again. And Mum and me, we'll look after you, alright?" As I was speaking, his eyes twinkled at me, I was certain of it. It was like he was trying to show me he was happy, as if he was saying thank you. It gave me the shivers to think that this plaster gnome could actually be listening to me, that he could really understand, that he had feelings. But they were nice shivers.

I couldn't be sure of it, but as I walked away with a half of him under each arm, I honestly thought I heard him chuckling – the top half of him and the bottom half at the same time. It was weird, but I liked it.

CHAPTER TWO

In which I put Mister Skip together again

I had to keep Mister Skip a secret. I didn't want Mum knowing anything about him, not until I'd put him together, not until her birthday. So I used the lock-up garage. We didn't have a car, but we did have a leaky lock-up where Mum never went, but I did. I went there whenever I wanted to be alone. It was my secret den, a bit smelly and dark and damp, but one end of it stayed dry, mostly. I'd made it as comfy as I could. I had a table in there under the window at the back and a chair and a bit of old carpet – all scrounged from the skip of course. So that's where I hid Mister Skip. That's where I planned to fix him up, and he needed an awful lot of fixing.

For a start there were some bits of him missing completely – one of his little hands and the top of his red bobble hat. I found the missing hand in the skip, in amongst someone's disgustingly slimy rubbish bags. I looked and looked, but I never did find the bit of his hat. It took me a couple of days, but in the end I managed to borrow some glue from the art cupboard at school, and some paints and some brushes. I told my teacher, Miss Munroe, that they were for a project I was working on at home. She seemed a little surprised at my sudden enthusiasm for art, and asked if she could see whatever it was I was working on when it was finished. "Maybe we could have it in the art exhibition for Parents' Evening, Jackie," she said. But she soon forgot all about it – thank goodness.

So now I had all I needed to put Mister Skip back together again. But I had to work fast. It was now only twelve days till Mum's birthday, and I wanted to make him perfect for her. I wanted him to look just how he must have done before he became all neglected and battered and broken in half.

First of all I scrubbed him down with a nailbrush. Then, when he was dry, I glued him back together, top half to bottom half, and I gave him back his missing hand. I filled his holes and cracks with Polyfilla and sanded down all his chips and scratches. Then I began to paint him, trying as best as I could to match the colours that were already there. His chubby cheeks had to be bright pink and his beard had to be white as white. He looked a bit like a mini Father Christmas, I thought, on a toadstool. His hat I painted bright red, his little boots too; and all his buttons had to be sparkling silver. I pinched some of Mum's special nail varnish for that – she didn't miss it. As for his trousers they should have been blue, but I couldn't find any blue paint in the art cupboard, so I made them green instead. And I made the toadstool look more like a toadstool again. Then I varnished him all over so that the paint would never come off.

By the time I was finished he was without any doubt the smartest shiniest garden gnome in all the world. All that had to be fixed now was the missing bit of his bobble hat. In the end I decided the best thing to do was to cover it up with a real hat. I did a swap with Barry: my Harry Potter sweatshirt – the one Gran gave to me for Christmas that had a hole in it – for his Liverpool red woolly hat, also with a hole in it. It fitted Mister Skip perfectly, and he looked really pleased with it too.

That was the strange thing about Mister Skip. Every day I worked on him he seemed to look happier and happier, so happy sometimes that I thought he really might burst out laughing. He never did. I mean he couldn't, could he? After all he was only plaster, I knew that. But sometimes after we'd been alone together in the lock-up for a while, I came to think of him almost as a real, live person. I suppose that was why I began talking to him – it just seemed natural somehow.

I told him all about Mum and me, our whole life story, about school, about Barry and Marty, about the Crazy Cossacks, about everything. He knew things about me I'd never even told Mum. He'd never say anything back of course. But once or twice I thought I heard a chuckling inside the lock-up when I left it to go home.

There were a couple of days still before Mum's birthday, and after school I'd spend all the time I could in the lock-up with Mister Skip. I'd just sit there admiring him, admiring my amazing handiwork, and looking forward to seeing the look on Mum's face when I gave him to her on her birthday. But then I began to think about him, about what was going on inside his head. I couldn't help wondering how lonely and miserable he must be left alone in the lock-up most of the day and all night without me.

I realised I was beginning to think of him not as a painted garden gnome at all, but as a friend who I liked to be with and who seemed to like being with me. Silly, I know, but that's how I felt.

It was on the last evening before Mum's birthday, and I was sitting there with Mister Skip in the lock-up just chatting away like I did, about how one day I would beat Barry and all the rest of the Crazy Cossacks out of sight, how I was going to wipe the floor with them. "I'll show them," I was saying. "I will too, honest. You watch me."

As usual Mister Skip just sat there smiling at me and never saying a word. But that was the thing. Suddenly I found myself almost expecting he would say something. He didn't. So I just went on gabbling. "Mister Skip, d'you know what Mum and I want more than anything else? First we want to build stables for all the horses on the estate, so they don't get all cold and miserable in the winter. Then we want to get off this lousy place. We're always on about it, always dreaming. We'd like a little house of our own in the country where there's green fields all around and hills and big wide skies, and no high buildings. And she'll keep chickens and ducks, and I'll have my own horse. I don't care what he's like really. Four legs and a tail, that's all I want. I'm not fussy, so long as he goes fast. I want to gallop out over the hills, splash through the rivers, jump the hedges.

I get all sad sometimes, Mister Skip, because I know it'll never happen. But like Mum says, it costs nothing to dream. Dreams are good for us, she says, they keep our spirits up. And she's right too. I can close my eyes whenever I like, and be out there in the country riding along, the wind in my face. Wouldn't it just be great?"

"Well, Jackie, d'you know what I'm thinking?" He spoke! I'm telling you, Mister Skip spoke! His lips never moved, but he spoke. Words came out. I heard them. He was speaking to me! He knew my name! For a few moments I was so stunned that I couldn't think straight  at all. Mister Skip went on. "Like I was saying, Jackie, I've been thinking that one good turn deserves another. Out of the kindness of your heart you picked me out of that skip, put me together again, and gave an old gnome a new lease of life. So I'll see to it that all your dreams will come true, and mine too come to that – I've got dreams of my own, y'know. But it's our secret, right? No-one else must know about it, just you and me. You never heard me. I never spoke a word, did I?"

I couldn't say anything. I just shook my head. "There's my girl. And Jackie, don't worry. It may not happen just as you think it'll happen, not even as you want it to happen, but it'll happen all the same. Promise."

His lips did not move as he spoke. None of him moved. But by the way Mister Skip looked at me, I knew for sure that he had spoken every single word, that I had imagined nothing.

I didn't sleep a wink that night. I kept expecting Mister Skip to come knocking at my window, or to find him sitting at the end of my bed. I was so tired at breakfast that I forgot to wish Mum a happy birthday. So, to remind me, she hummed "happy birthday" very loudly and very deliberately as she buttered my toast. I gave her a big birthday hug and she forgave me. I said I'd give her her present at teatime, and then off I went to school. On the way I checked the lock-up to be sure Mister Skip was still there. He was sitting just where I'd left him on the table under the window, not speaking, but smiling.

"Mister Skip," I whispered. "About yesterday. Did you really talk to me? Did you?" All I heard in reply was the drip drip of the water as it came through the roof in the corner, and my own tummy gurgling – I hadn't eaten my breakfast.

At school, I couldn't think of anything else except Mister Skip and all he'd said to me. Miss Munroe gave me a ticking off for daydreaming, and then a detention for doodling in my English book. We were supposed to be writing a story about a giraffe, and all I'd written was "Mister Skip. Mister Skip. Mister Skip". And I'd done a dozen or more drawings of garden gnomes.

"Who's this Mister Skip?" Miss Munroe had said, waving my exercise book in my face. "And what are these drawings, Jackie?" I didn't even know I'd been doing them. "They're not even giraffes, Jackie. They're garden gnomes. What have you got to say for yourself?" I just shrugged. She hates it when we shrug. That's why I had to stay in at playtime.

During storytime in the afternoon I was so
tired I dropped off to sleep. But even when I
was asleep, all I dreamed of was Mister
Skip. He was talking to me again, telling me
how I'd win all the races I wanted to. After
school, after Miss Munroe had kept me
behind to tick me off again, I ran all the way
back to the lock-up. I don't know why, but I
had this terrible premonition inside me, that

I'd find him gone when I got there, that he might have just opened the door and gone, and worse still that maybe someone might have broken in and stolen him.

As I came round the corner I saw that every one of the lock-ups was shut. So I needn't have worried after all. But then I opened the lock-up door. He was gone. Mister Skip was gone.

CHAPTER THREE

In which Barnaby comes to stay

All sorts of wild thoughts went racing through my mind. First I thought that maybe Mister Skip had really got up and walked out, closing the door behind him. No, that was impossible. Then I thought that maybe I'd imagined the whole thing, dreamed it up in my head: the finding of Mister Skip, the mending of Mister Skip, the talking of Mister Skip. But the paint and the brushes were still there on the table. So it couldn't be that.

"Someone's pinched him," I said it out loud, and I knew this was more than likely. Things were always going "missing" on our estate — car wheels, lampposts, a whole telephone box once. But whatever had happened Mister Skip had vanished. I sat down at the table and cried my heart out. I had lost more than a plaster garden gnome. I had lost a friend, someone I could talk to. Worst of all, I'd lost Mum's birthday present, and I had nothing else to give her.

I don't know how long I sat there, but it must have been a while, because as I was climbing the stairs up to the flat, I met Mum coming down the other way, coming to look for me. "I've been so worried, Jackie," she cried. "Where've you been?"

I didn't know what to say, so I said nothing.

Mum took me by the hand and walked me up the stairs chatting on as we went. "You won't believe what happened to me today, Jackie. First I had this phone call from your Aunty Mary. Your gran's been worrying herself sick about that old donkey of hers, that Barnaby. You know that hip operation Gran's been waiting for all these months?

Well, the hospital finally called, and said they could have her in right away. But Gran wouldn't go into hospital unless she could find someone to look after Barnaby. Your Aunty Mary couldn't have him on account of her having her animal allergy, so she rings me and says will we look after him for a few weeks. I said it was a bit awkward, looking after a donkey, living as we do six floors up in a two bedroom flat. But she wouldn't listen, you know what she's like." We'd just about reached the sixth floor by now and I was puffed out. "And then I thought how

39

much you love looking after Barnaby whenever we go for holidays to Gran's place, and how you're always on about having a horse of your own. Well, a donkey's pretty close to a horse, I thought, and we could stable him in the lock-up, and you could muck him out. You like mucking out, don't you? We could manage. So I said yes. He'll be here tomorrow morning, Jackie. Isn't that great? Then I go down to the lock-up just to check it out – haven't been down there for years – just to make sure no-one's pinched the door. And what d'you think I find, Jackie?"

I knew alright. I knew. "I don't know," I said.

"Someone's only been in there, in our lock-up. They've only been using it as a workshop. And there's this... you're not going to believe this..." I am, Mum, I am.

"You could've knocked me down with a feather. Gave me the shock of my life." We'd reached the door of the flat by now and she made me close my eyes. "Surprise," she said, and led me into the kitchen. "Alright, Jackie, you can open them now." And of course there was Mister Skip sitting on the kitchen table by the tomato sauce, and smiling at me very knowingly.

"Isn't he just incredible!" Mum went on. "Finders keepers, that's what I say. He was in our lock-up, wasn't he? So he's ours. Mine."

"Yes, Mum," I said. "He's your birthday present from me." And then I told her everything. Well, not everything. I left out the bit about Mister Skip talking to me. After all, that was our private secret. Mum went all weepy on me, and squeezed me so tight I could hardly breathe. As she hugged me there in the kitchen and told me how wonderful I was, Mister Skip was looking right at me and smiling. I longed to ask him if old Barnaby coming to stay had anything to do with his promise that I'd win at the races. But I couldn't imagine how. I couldn't ask him either, not until Mum went out later to get us our fish and chips. But when at last she'd gone and I sat down and asked him about it, all he did was smile at me. I decided to tell him about Barnaby, just so he would know. "Listen, Mister Skip," I said. "I don't know what you're playing at, but if you think I'm riding Barnaby at the races, you can think again. He's the slowest, sleepiest donkey that was ever born. I know. I've known him all my life. All he does is walk. He won't even trot, and he certainly won't run. So if Barnaby's part of your big plan, forget it." But Mister Skip just kept on smiling.

"It's not funny," I told him.

"I'm not laughing, Jackie," he said suddenly. "I smile even when I'm serious. It's just how I am. And I'm serious about my promises. I always keep them. You'll see." And no matter how often I asked him, he wouldn't say another word. He sat there all the way through supper still not saying a word. And neither did I. I didn't feel like eating my fish and chips either. I was too worried.

"You alright, Jackie?" Mum asked me. I said I was just tired and went off to bed early. When she came in later to say good night, I could tell she was really happy with her present. "What'll we call him?" she said, as she tucked me in.

"Mister Skip," I told her.

"Perfect," she said. "There's something about Mister Skip. It's the way he looks at you, like he's listening almost."

I really wanted to tell her everything, that Mister Skip doesn't just listen, but that he talks too. But I couldn't. I just couldn't. It would sound so mad, so silly. And hadn't I promised Mister Skip it would be our secret? It was hard, but I kept my promise and I didn't tell her.

"We'll have to get the lock-up ready for Barnaby," she went on. "He'll have to graze with the horses by day and we'll bring him into the lock-up at night-time."

"They'll laugh at him," I told her. "Everyone will. I know they will."

"He's a lovely old donkey," she said. "Course they won't laugh at him."

But they did. Word soon got about that Jackie Dawson's donkey would be arriving that afternoon, so that by the time the horsebox came half the estate was there, including Marty and Barry and all the Crazy Cossacks. As Barnaby came slowly backwards down the ramp, they were all tittering and laughing. Barnaby had never looked so scruffy in all his life, like a dirty old brown carpet on four hairy legs. His ears were turning this way and that, and I could tell how

upset he was getting. I could see he was wondering why they were laughing at him, wondering what this strange place was, wondering where Gran was, where his lovely green fields were. I went up to him and put my arms round his neck. "It's alright, Barnaby," I told him. "I'll look after you. It's alright. We've got a nice stable all ready for you."

"Eeeeaw! Eeeeaw!" Marty Morgan chanted, and then the rest of them started up, all the Crazy Cossacks. "Eeeeaw! Eeeeaw! Eeeeaw!"

That was it. I'd had enough. Now I was really mad. I turned on them and told them just what I thought of them. But I didn't stop there. "I'll give you eeeeaw," I shouted. "I'm telling you Barnaby can beat the lot of you, you and all your fancy horses and ponies. He goes like the wind, so he does." I could not believe what I was saying, and nor could anyone else. They were all gaping at me. I mean I never say things like that, not to anyone, and certainly not to Marty Morgan – I've never been that brave. But I'd said it. It was like it wasn't me doing the talking at all, but whoever it was doing the talking hadn't finished yet. "Not that you'll dare race me of course. You'll make up some feeble excuse about girls not being allowed to ride in the races or something. But that's because you're chicken, the whole lousy lot of you are chicken."

You could have heard a pin drop. And then Marty Morgan said it. "Alright, you're on. Tomorrow afternoon. Saturday. The big race. The Crazy Cossacks will be waiting for you, won't we lads?" And away they went eeeeawing and giggling and guffawing, leaving me feeling very stupid and very alone.

But then Mum started up and I didn't feel alone any more. "You just wait!" she shouted. "This isn't just any old donkey, y'know. This is a Ferrari of a donkey, a Concorde of a donkey. He's turbocharged, y'hear me, turbocharged!"

That's the great thing about Mum. In front of other people she always sticks by me, whatever. She waited till everyone was gone, and then she started on me. "What is it with you, Jackie? Are you mad in the head, or what? Barnaby can't race. He can't even run. You know he can't. He's just a stubborn old donkey, not a race horse. You won't get him off the start line. You know what he does if you try to make him do anything he doesn't want to do, he just sits down."

She was right, too. I knew exactly what Barnaby would do if I tried to kick him on. He would sit down like a dog, and there'd be no way I'd ever get him up again.

"I couldn't help myself, Mum," I said. "When they began laughing at Barnaby, the words just came pouring out." That was the truth of it too. Suddenly I knew how it had all happened. It hadn't been me speaking at all, it had been Mister Skip. He'd put the words in my mouth and somehow he'd made me say them. Then I began to think, began to hope, that maybe if Mister Skip could make one kind of magic, then maybe, just maybe he could make another kind, and make Barnaby win the race tomorrow. Maybe he wouldn't sit down. Maybe he'd actually run, run and win. But I knew in my heart it was only wishful thinking, that there was no way Barnaby could possibly win, not in a million years. "You will come and cheer me on, Mum?" I asked nervously.

."Wild horses wouldn't keep me away, Jackie," she replied. "Me and you against the world, right? I'll be with you all the way, win or lose. And I'll be cheering too. Louder than anyone. But I reckon we'll need more than cheering, Jackie. We need a miracle. That's what we need, a miracle."

CHAPTER FOUR

In which Barnaby goes to the Saturday races

The next morning early I went down to the lock-up in my dressing gown and fed Barnaby his hay. He ate like a horse. I just hoped he would run like one too. I came back afterwards and ate my own breakfast in silence, Mister Skip watching every mouthful of toast and strawberry jam as it went in.

Mum tried her best to cheer me up, but it was no use. I could see it all in my mind. I could hear it all – all their prancing dancing ponies tossing their heads at the start line, pawing the ground, then dashing off into the distance, the Crazy Cossacks' mocking laughter ringing in my ears, and me miles behind, barely able to get old Barnaby to walk.

Mum was at the fridge fetching some milk when suddenly and quite definitely Mister Skip began to chuckle. She turned round, so surprised that she nearly dropped the milk carton.

"What was that?" she said.

"My tummy, Mum," I said. "It's my tummy rumbling. Nerves. I'm awful nervous." The chuckling stopped, thank goodness, as Mum came back to the table.

"It'll be alright, Jackie," she said, stroking my hair. "Don't you worry yourself." Then she sat down and patted Mister Skip on his head. "I do love my birthday present. Always smiling he is, no matter what. It's almost like there's three of us now, three of us against the world."

I knew it would make no difference, but before I took Barnaby out I groomed him till he looked a little less like a dirty old carpet and a little bit more like a new one. I picked out his feet, brushed his tail, and stroked his ears – he always liked me to do that back at Gran's. The last thing I did inside the lock-up was to whisper into his ear: "Please Barnaby. Just for once in your life, go fast, go like the wind. Please. Please."

Then I led him out of the lock-up, out onto the green where they were all gathering, and I mean *all*. Everyone on the estate must have been there, and I knew why. They all knew by now that Barnaby was going to run in the big Saturday race and they'd all come for a good laugh. There was always a good turnout for the Saturday race. It was a well-known event. People would come from miles around to see it. But I'd never in my life seen a crowd like this. There must have been hundreds of people milling around, thousands even, and all the Crazy Cossacks' ponies and horses were racing up and down showing their paces.

Barnaby just stopped dead. He didn't like what he saw at all, any more than I did. I smoothed his neck and patted him. "It'll be alright, Barnaby," I whispered. But then the Crazy Cossacks spotted us. They were pointing at us and eeeeawing, the whole horrible lot of them – except Barry who, to be fair, did look a bit shamefaced. The whole crowd seemed to be laughing. I felt like turning tail and running. But suddenly Mum was there beside me, leading out Barnaby with me, and all the while she was waving to the crowd like we were coming into the winner's enclosure at the Irish Derby. Mum was brilliant, utterly brilliant. Very soon they weren't laughing at us any more, they were clapping instead. Then they were cheering. Barnaby knew it too. He was suddenly enjoying it. He was up on his toes, his ears pricked forward. At one point he even broke into a brief little trot. I could hardly believe it.

It made me feel a whole lot better too. Alright, so we would come in last, I knew that, but at least people would be cheering us and not laughing at us. That would be enough for me.

It was my fault that Barnaby sat down.

When the race started and the others went galloping off, Barnaby was just left standing. All I did was give him the gentlest of kicks with my heels to get him going. A little tickle that's all it was. "Go!" I shouted. I shouldn't have done it. I shouldn't have said it. I knew well enough that if you kick Barnaby on, he

sits down. He'd done it to me dozens of times when I was at Gran's place on holiday. But I forgot I suppose, or I just didn't think. Anyway he sat down, and I slid off the back of him, and sat there on the ground feeling very stupid, and very angry with myself for being so stupid.

I expected everyone to laugh, but they didn't. I think maybe they felt sorry for me. Mum helped me up, and said it didn't matter one bit, that I'd soon catch up with the others. Once up on Barnaby again I took the reins and looked up ahead of me. There wasn't a horse in sight. I felt like giving up, but something inside me made me do what I should have done in the first place. You don't *tell* Barnaby what to do, you ask him nicely. "Please Barnaby," I whispered in his ear. "Do it for Mister Skip." Well, that did it. It was as if some hugely powerful electrical charge suddenly surged through him. He seemed to stiffen and grow underneath me. He tossed his head like a bull. He pawed the ground like a stallion. He blew and he snorted like a whale. He let out a great eeeeaw that echoed round the estate, and then off he went. I went with him but only just. I clung on round his neck. It was all I could do. Barnaby wasn't trotting. He wasn't cantering. He was galloping. He was fairly flying over the ground, his hoof beats thundering.

I had no time to think about falling off, no time to be frightened. I'd lost my reins by now, so there was no way I could guide him. But that didn't seem to matter. He knew the way. Within no time I could see the Crazy Cossacks up ahead, and Barnaby could see them too. He didn't need telling. He was after them.

The rush of the wind on my face took my breath away. I was so happy, so exhilarated. I felt like whooping and cheering, but I couldn't find the voice to do it. And all the time I was catching up with the Crazy Cossacks. Nearer. Nearer. Nearer.

Not one of them looked back. No-one was

expecting me. As I passed the Crazy Cossacks one by one, all they could do was gape at me in sheer disbelief. But Marty Morgan and Barry were still out there in the lead, neck and neck, and were way ahead of me. I was coming up fast, but not fast enough. I could see the winning post now and the crowd leaping up and down, and Mum yelling louder than anyone. I don't know how I thought of it – because I was far too tired to think – but I breathed into Barnaby's ear what I hoped were the magic words: "Please, Barnaby, do it for Mister Skip." They were magic alright.

Barnaby seemed to slip instantly up into an even higher gear. He may have been puffing and blowing like an old steam engine, but was he going! We cruised past Marty and Barry, and as we passed them I just smiled at them. It was the happiest smile of my entire life, and a smile that stayed with me all the way to the finishing post. I punched the air in triumph. I had it in mind that as soon as Barnaby stopped I would do a Frankie Dettori jump-off. But Barnaby didn't stop. He charged straight on scattering the cheering crowd as he went, and straight back towards his lock-up. Just outside he stopped very suddenly, too suddenly. I went flying over his head and landed in a pile of bin bags, that luckily for me were full, so that although I was shaken and a bit smelly, I wasn't at all hurt.

I was still lying there in amongst the bin bags and trying to collect my thoughts when Mum and everyone came running. She helped me to my feet and made sure I was alright. We just hugged and cried and hugged some more.

And she wasn't the only one hugging me. It seemed everyone on the estate thought I was the bee's knees. Miss Munroe from school was there. She hugged me too! Who didn't hug me? Well, the Crazy Cossacks didn't. Marty Morgan certainly didn't. Instead they hung around for a while shaking their heads and looking all bewildered and sorry for themselves. Barry managed to mutter a "well done", which was as good as a dozen hugs to me. He even stayed behind and helped me towel Barnaby down and groom him. Then he said Barnaby could spend the rest of the day grazing with Dasher on the green, if I wanted.

We were walking Barnaby up there some time later when this big car came up alongside us, and a young man leaned out and said: "Is that the superdonkey that runs faster than horses?"

"Yes," I replied.

"Well, I'm from the newspaper. Can I have a photo and a bit of a chat?"

It didn't take long, a couple of photos of Barnaby and me and a few questions about the race. That's all it was.

I told Mum all about the reporter when I got home. We were having fish and chips – again, to celebrate. We sat there, Mum and me, in the kitchen, scoffing down our fish and chips, and going over the race again and again, and all the time Mister Skip was watching us both. I couldn't stop looking at him. I knew, I just knew, that somehow he had made it all happen. It was difficult with Mum there, but I felt I had to say thank you to him. I couldn't just sit there and say nothing. So after I'd said good night to Mum, I said it to him too. "G'night, Mister Skip," I said, "and thanks." And I kissed him on both his pink cheeks.

"What are you thanking him for?" Mum

laughed. "It was Barnaby who won that race, Barnaby and you."

"I can't explain it, Mum," I said. "I just think he's lucky for us somehow, that's all."

"A sort of lucky mascot, you mean?" Mum said.

"Something like that," I replied, and went off to bed. I lay there in the dark wondering what would happen tomorrow or the next day, knowing now for sure that Mister Skip had already made one of my dreams come true. I knew that whatever happened next, Mister Skip would be behind it. Somehow, Mister Skip would be pulling the strings. Barnaby and me, we were just puppets. But I didn't mind, I didn't mind at all.

CHAPTER FIVE

In which Mister Skip has a cunning plan

Next Monday there we were, Barnaby and me with our picture all over the front page of the newspaper – "Superdonk wins the day at the races". Mum rang up Gran in hospital. She rang up Aunty Mary. She rang everyone she could think of. Then she dashed out to buy a dozen copies of the paper. While she was gone I just sat there shovelling in my Weetabix and looking at the photo again and again. Me and Barnaby in the paper. I just couldn't believe it.

"You'd better believe it," said a voice. Mister Skip. I'd almost forgotten about him. "You'd almost forgotten about me, hadn't you?" he said. He could read my mind too! "Listen Jackie, a lot's going to happen in the next few days. I want you to remember just one thing. However impossible it sounds, just say you'll do it. Alright?"

"But what do you mean? What's going to happen?"

"No questions, Jackie. Do it for Mister Skip, eh? Like Barnaby did."

We didn't have time to talk any more because Mum came back all excited and breathless and piled high with newspapers.

"Everyone's seen it, Jackie," she said. "Everyone's talking about it, about the race, about you and Barnaby."

And she was right. I had more friends walking with me to school that day than I'd ever had before. When I got into the playground I was mobbed. Everyone asked me questions at the same time. "How did he do it, Jackie?" "What did you put in his food, Jackie?" "How did you make a donkey go that fast?"

Luckily they didn't give me time to answer, because I had no answers to give – none I could tell them anyway. I hadn't a clue how Mister Skip had made it all happen. All I knew was that it was him that had done it – and that was our secret.

In Assembly our headteacher, Mrs Tandy, waved the newspaper in front of everyone and read out the article. Then she said that Barnaby was a star, and I was a star. Suddenly I had a nickname. I had become Jackie Dettori. Of course I got a few looks from Marty Morgan and some of his Crazy Cossacks, but I didn't mind, not one bit. I tried not to look too happy, but it was difficult because I was right up there on cloud nine.

In the lunch break I was called into Mrs Tandy's office. And there was Barnaby *in her office*! Mum was there too, and Mrs

Tandy was offering Barnaby an apple which he didn't want. He looked very fed up. "They're waiting for us, Jackie," said Mum. Mum was made up like I'd never seen her before – lipstick, eyeshadow, mascara, the lot. And her hair, she'd had her hair done! She was grinning like a cat that just got the cream, a cat with scarlet lipstick. Practically purring she was.

"Who is?" I asked. "Who's waiting for us?"

"Only the TV cameras! They want you to put Barnaby through his paces for them. They want to film him, and you too. You'll be on the telly, on the news!"

But all I could think was: what if Barnaby wouldn't do it a second time? What if he didn't go off like a turbo-charged donkey? What if he didn't go off at all?

"And Mrs Tandy's said it's fine, Jackie," Mum went on. "She says she'll bring along the whole school to cheer you on. Isn't that just great?" Barnaby decided at that moment to take the apple and Mrs Tandy's finger in the same bite.

"Eeeaaaeee!" Mrs Tandy shrieked, and then tried to laugh it off. "He's got a terrible powerful bite."

"He's a terrible powerful donkey, Mrs Tandy," said Mum, bursting with pride.

"What's up, Jackie? You don't look well."

I didn't feel well. I felt like running off there and then, legging it home, but then I heard Mister Skip's voice in my head. "However impossible it sounds, just say you'll do it." So I said "I'll do it."

Less than half an hour later, there I was mounted up on Barnaby, with the whole school looking on and the woman from the telly interviewing me. It seemed like half the world was gathered there on the estate, watching and waiting. I tried to concentrate. Don't kick him on, I was thinking. Don't touch him with your heels, or he'll sit down. Ask him, ask him nicely like you did before. So when the interviewing was over and the cameras were ready, I bent down over his neck and whispered the magic words in his ear, "Do it for Mister Skip, Barnaby."

His ears twitched, first one, then the other. And suddenly he was off, off from the start, like a race horse. If anything he was going faster than before, and like before all I could do was hold on and pray I didn't fall off.

There wasn't time to enjoy it. I just clung on and hoped. Even when we'd done the circuit round the estate, and were galloping towards the crowds and the cameras, I still couldn't enjoy it because all the time I just had this feeling Barnaby was going to do what he'd done before. He was going to dump me. And so he did, and he chose the same place too. He ran on past the crowd, stopped dead in his tracks by his lock-up stable and dumped me again in the same old

smelly bin bags. Everyone loved that of course, but now they loved me too – even the Crazy Cossacks. It was Marty and Barry and the others who hoisted me up on their shoulders and carried me off in triumph. Unbelievable!

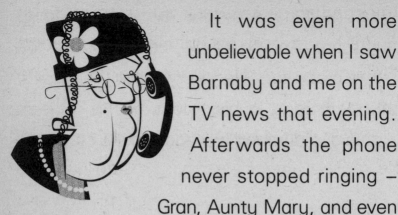

It was even more unbelievable when I saw Barnaby and me on the TV news that evening. Afterwards the phone never stopped ringing – Gran, Aunty Mary, and even total strangers. And people from the flats all around kept coming round and telling us they'd just seen us on the telly. They'd bring a bottle and in they'd come. It was one long party, and Mum was loving every minute of it. But after a while I got a bit fed up with all the noise and the questions and I went off to my room, taking Mister Skip with me.

Anyway, I wanted a little private chat, just him and me.

I needed some answers. So I set him down on my bed and asked him straight out: "What's going on, Mister Skip? What are you up to?"

"Well, that'd be telling, wouldn't it now," he replied, chuckling away inside himself. "Let's just say I've a cunning plan in my head that could make things right for you Jackie, and for me too with a little bit of luck. Don't you go worrying yourself about it. Things'll work themselves out just fine." And when I tried to ask more, all he did was sit there smiling at me and saying nothing, not a word. I couldn't even get a chuckle out of him.

As it turned out I didn't have long to wait to see what Mister Skip had in store for me. Later that same evening, when everything had calmed down a bit, I went down to the lock-up to groom Barnaby. I was making sure he had enough hay and water to keep him happy through the night, when Barry and Marty came looking for me, along with the other Crazy Cossacks. They were all puffed out with running.

"Have you heard?" said Barry excitedly.

"What?" I asked.

"About the big race," Marty said.

"What big race?" I hadn't a clue what they were on about.

"They're calling it the Barnaby Derby," Marty explained, his words tumbling out so fast they were falling over each other. "But it's not for any old donkeys. It's just for Barnaby. It'll be Barnaby against the best race horses in the whole world, from Ireland, America, England." Now they were all telling me at the same time, so I couldn't understand anything. In the end it was Barry who shut them all up and told me. "They timed him, Jackie. They timed Barnaby this afternoon. From some newspaper or other they were. That donkey of yours was going over forty miles an hour! Can you believe that? Forty miles an hour. That's as fast as any race horse. So the newspaper's sent out a challenge to all the best race horse stables in the world. It was on the telly just now! Has anyone got a horse that can beat Barnaby, the superdonkey?! And wait for it, Jackie. There's a prize for the winner, a big prize, a very big prize, a humungously big prize."

"How much?" I asked.

"Only a million euros. A million euros," said Marty. "Can you believe it?"

Oh yes, I could believe it. By now I could believe anything, absolutely anything. Of course they were all expecting me to be surprised. But I wasn't, not one bit. All I knew was that Mister Skip was up to his tricks. I could see what he was up to alright, but the whole thing was mad, impossible, ridiculous, wonderful!

"Well," said Marty. "What d'you think? Can he beat the best in the world? Can you win the million?"

"Course," said my voice, only I wasn't doing the speaking. "Why not? No problem." It was Mister Skip doing the speaking for me again. Well that silenced them. They just stood there and gawped at me, and I carried on filling Barnaby's haynet, cool as a cucumber – on the outside, that is. But on the inside I was screaming. Barnaby against the best race horses in the world! Are you off your trolley or what, Mister Skip?

Mum was alone in the kitchen washing up

when I got back up to the flat. Everyone else was gone. I could tell she hadn't heard, that no one had told her. I mean she wasn't leaping up and down, was she? And I could see from the smug smile on Mister Skip's face that he didn't need to be told a thing, nothing at all.

"Mum," I began. "I've got some news." And then I told her.

"A million euros?" she breathed, leaning back against the sink to steady herself. "A million smackeroos?"

"Yep," I said.

"Can you do it? Can Barnaby do it?"

"Yep," I said again. And she threw her soapsudsy hands in the air, and danced around the room, whooping like a mad thing. "Jackie, oh Jackie! We can have our dreams. They can all come true; the stables for the horses, my house in the country, my chickens and ducks, a horse of your own." And she hugged me so tight I thought I'd break. Over her shoulder I saw Mister Skip, sitting there on the table, smiling at me with "I told you so" written all over his chubby little face. His eyes were telling me: "You can do it, Jackie, you can do it." And suddenly I believed I could too and I was smiling right back at him.

CHAPTER SIX

In which Magnus Finnegan lends us a helping hand

The Barnaby Derby took a couple of months to set up. There was a lot of fuss and bother of course, which was great. I mean, I was famous now, really famous, and so was Barnaby. Not Madonna famous, but not far off. And that was all because of Mister Skip of course, and Magnus Finnegan. It was

Magnus Finnegan that looked after us through the whole thing.

I won't forget the day Magnus Finnegan turned up on our estate in his limousine. It was long, and low and snow-white, with blacked-out windows. When he got out he was puffing the biggest fattest cigar I ever saw. He was a film producer, from America he said, and wanted to see me riding out on Barnaby to see for himself if all he'd heard was true. So of course I just whispered the magic words: "Do it for Mister Skip" in Barnaby's ear, and off he went. I'd done it often enough now by this time to look all super cool and confident when I was riding him, and I'd taught him long ago not to stop too suddenly, and not to dump me in the bin bags either. Magnus Finnegan and Mum stood side by side and watched. When I'd

finished, Magnus Finnegan took his cigar out
of his mouth and just said one word: "Wow!"
Then he and Mum and the driver went up to
the flat to have a cup of tea, and to "talk
turkey", he said – whatever that meant, while
I put Barnaby back out to grass. Whatever
they talked about didn't take that long. They
both came out smiling, so they must have got
on well with their "talking turkey", I thought.

After that it was Magnus Finnegan who organised everything; the radio, the television, all the newspaper interviews and photo shoots. They came from all over the world; Japan, Australia, America, France – everywhere. But no-one got near us for an interview unless Magnus Finnegan said so. He was a good friend to us and we liked him, except that his cigars stank.

All this time Mister Skip never said a word. He just sat there in the kitchen and smiled and let it all happen. When we were alone, I'd ask him again and again if he was sure we really could beat the best race horses in the world, if we really could win the million euro prize. He never so much as chuckled. I thought he wrinkled his nose and coughed when Magnus Finnegan was smoking his cigar, but otherwise he behaved just like any ordinary plaster garden gnome.

Once I got so fed up with him just smiling and not answering me that I put the drying-up cloth over his head. Mum came in and took it off. "You shouldn't do that, Jackie," she said. "You think about it. Ever since you brought him here, we've had nothing but good luck." How I wanted to tell Mum all about him, all about Mister Skip's cunning plan, but I thought that if I did, it might somehow break the magic.

The great day came at last. Early in the morning I groomed Barnaby in the lock-up like he'd never been groomed before. He looked as good as I could make him. After breakfast I said goodbye to Mister Skip and asked him to wish me luck, but he didn't. He smiled instead – of course. I knew that when I saw him the next time, we'd be a million euros richer. So I put my arms round his neck and thanked him in advance. Then we boxed up Barnaby and drove off in Magnus Finnegan's limousine to the race course – the Curragh they call it. It's only the place where they run the Irish Derby!

We had a police escort all the way, and there were crowds of people everywhere. They couldn't see us through the blackened windows of the limousine, but I could see them, and I could make faces at them too, without being seen at all. Mum led Barnaby round in the parade ring. All made up like a queen she was and waving like one too. And all around us were the finest horses you could ever hope to see, shining and sleek in the sunlight, all up on their tippy toes, tossing their fancy heads, raring to be off. One or two took fright at Barnaby and bolted. Marty and Barry, and all the Crazy Cossacks

were there. Gran was there too, waving, all better now after her operation, and Aunty Mary too in a great yellow hat – she looked a bit as if a huge lemon meringue pie had fallen splat on her head.

For me it was just the best feeling in the world. I was up there now on Barnaby and riding out of the enclosure, Mum and everyone watching me and hoping I would win. They'd dressed me up like a regular jockey with a bright pink shirt and a matching pink hat, so I looked the part. I felt the part too as I trotted up to the start. I wasn't hoping I would win. I knew I would.

Then we were off. Well to be exact, *they* were off. At that moment Barnaby decided he would eat the grass. I wasn't worried. I knew he could catch them up. I just whispered the magic words: "Do it for Mister Skip." But Barnaby went on eating. Perhaps he hadn't heard me. I said it louder: "Do it for Mister Skip, Barnaby." Barnaby went on eating. I looked up. The horses were already racing round the first bend, and still Barnaby hadn't moved. Then I panicked, and I did a foolish thing. I kicked Barnaby, only gently,

just a little touch of my heels to gee him up, and he sat down. He sat down, and I slid off the back of him and landed with a bump on my bottom. So now there were two of us sitting there. When I'd got over the shock of it I jumped up and tried to haul him to his feet. He looked at me, and his eyes told me the worst: "I'm not moving, not for you, not for Mister Skip, not for anyone."

To cut a long story, and a sad story, short, Barnaby never budged, no matter what I did or what I said. I heard the crowd cheering as the horses came up the straight to the finish, and there I was still on my knees, begging and pleading. In the end, when it was all over, they had to send the horsebox out to pick us up. Barnaby went up the ramp easy as pie – I could have killed him – and then he eeeeawed happily in the back as we drove away from the race course, which was just as well because it helped drown out the booing of the crowd all around us.

All the way home in the limousine I could hardly see because my eyes were so full of tears. But Mum never stopped her chattering, and neither did Magnus Finnegan, who was chuckling just like Mister Skip. "Not to worry, Jackie," Mum said. "Don't be all down in the dumps. What's a million euros here or there? Easy come. Easy go. I mean, we never had it in the first place, did we? So we haven't lost anything, have we? And what d'you expect anyway? When all's said and done, a donkey will always be a donkey, if you see what I'm saying." Well, I didn't.

Magnus Finnegan chuckled somewhere behind the fog of his cigar smoke, and said, "Whichever way it ended, Jackie, it's still a great story. Believe me, in Hollywood, that's all that counts." I hadn't a clue what either of them were going on about.

No crowds were waiting for us when we got back home to the estate, no reporters, no television cameras. I led Barnaby into his lock-up where he began chomping happily on his hay. I was too angry with him even to speak to him, let alone brush him down. I just filled up his water bucket and left him there.

When I got up to the flat, Magnus Finnegan had gone, but I could still smell his filthy cigar smoke. Mum was making the tea. "I've done you toast and strawberry jam," she said, "your favourite." That was the moment I burst into tears. I sobbed my heart out and Mum just held me and stroked my hair. "A million euros, Mum," I wailed, and poured out all my miseries. "Barnaby just sat there. He wouldn't move. We could have had everything we always wanted, the house in the countryside, your chickens and ducks, a horse of my own. And we could have built stables for all the horses on the estate to keep them warm in the winter. It's all so unfair, Mum." I caught sight of Mister Skip looking at me. "And I wish," I went on, "I wish that stupid garden gnome would stop smiling at me."

"Don't go blaming him, Jackie," said Mum. "Mister Skip can't help it, he's always smiling. And besides, maybe he's smiling because he's happy. Like me. I'm happy. I'm smiling." And I could see she was too, from ear to ear. It was crazy. We'd just lost a million euros and she was happy.

"Close your eyes, Jackie," Mum said. I heard her go out of the kitchen, and so I opened them again. Mister Skip was sitting there smiling at me. I stuck my tongue out at him. I heard Mum coming back and closed my eyes again. I heard her moving the cups and plates aside, and putting something that sounded very heavy down on the table.

"Alright, Jackie," she said. "You can open them now."

It was her battered old leather suitcase – one I'd rescued from the skip some time before. "Take a deep breath, Jackie," she said, and then she opened it. It was stuffed full of money, twenty euro notes, fifty euro notes. "But how come you've got all that money?" I cried. "We lost!"

"So what?" said Mum. She was being deliberately mysterious and I still didn't understand. "All those reporter fellows, all those telly people. Did you really think I'd let them have something for nothing? Magnus. Magnus Finnegan, him with the big cigar and the car as long as the Titanic, I did a deal with Magnus right at the start, Jackie. He wanted to buy our story, your story, Barnaby's story, to make a film out of it. So I said fine, you pay us a great whack of money and look after us, and you can have our story, that'll be just fine. And now he's paid up. None of your cheques or your plastic card rubbish. Cash, ready money, the real stuff."

"How much?" I breathed.

"Only 500,000 smackeroos," said Mum. "It's not a million maybe, but who's counting? It'll be quite enough to buy us our own place in the country, and for a horse for yourself, and for a nice stable for all the horses on the estate. Enough is as good as a feast, that's what I say."

I didn't understand that either – not until Mister Skip explained it later. But after a moment or two of hard thinking I did begin to understand about the money and how she'd got it. 500,000 euros for a story, for our story! Maybe Barnaby would be in the movies! Maybe I'd be in the movies! I cried all over again, and so did Mum then, and we danced round the table laughing and crying both at the same time.

Later, when Mum had gone off to bed, I went back into the kitchen to have a quiet word with Mister Skip. "I thought you'd let me down, Mister Skip," I whispered.

"Would I do that to you, Jackie?" he replied. "There's ways and ways of doing things, and I thought this way would be more fun. And besides, when I thought about it, I thought maybe a million was too much money. So I changed my mind, and you lost the race. Winning isn't always good, Jackie, not all the time. And too much money, like too little, is not a good thing." I understood now, I understood perfectly.

"I don't know how to thank you," I told him.

"Aren't you forgetting something?" Mister Skip said. "Didn't you put me all back together again? Didn't you give me a new life? This is me thanking you, Jackie. Like I said, one good turn deserves another."

I reached out and I hugged him tight, before I left him chuckling away in the dark of the kitchen.

CHAPTER SEVEN

In which Mum has a cunning idea, and everything turns out just fine

So first of all we had twenty brand new stables put up on the edge of the estate for the horses. But we made Marty and Barry promise that from now on girls could join the Crazy Cossacks and ride in the Saturday race just the same as the boys. And a few months later we found our dream house with green fields all around it, on a beautiful hillside out in County Wicklow. There was enough room for Gran and Aunty Mary to have a room each when they came to stay and Mum could keep all the chickens and ducks she wanted. And when I looked out of my bedroom window now there were no concrete tower blocks, no roads, no cars, just a great big wide sky and grass and trees, and a winding stream and shifting sheep and Barnaby grazing in a field with a horse – my horse. I called him Skippy, of course. And he goes like the wind, of course.

Mister Skip himself lived outside by the front door – he told me that garden gnomes prefer to live outside. "It's where we belong," he said. So I often went and sat there on the front doorstep to talk to him. He'd always listen, I knew that, and he'd speak to me sometimes, but not as often as

I'd like. I began to get the feeling he was a bit sad all on his own out there.

Then one day Mum said she had a cunning idea. "I was thinking," she began, "I was thinking that Mister Skip looks a little lonely and sad out there all on his own."

"That's just what I was thinking," I told her.

"Great minds think alike," she said. "I was thinking that we could set up a sort of business, a little business that'll maybe bring in a bit of money, and one that'll keep Mister Skip happy at the same time. I reckon that, one way or another, that old gnome has done us a power of good. He's given you and me the best times we've ever had. And I'm thinking… one good turn… how does that saying go, Jackie?"

"One good turn deserves another?" I said.

"Right," said Mum.

And so it was that the very next day Mum put a big advertisement in the *Irish Times*. "Wanted. Any old gnomes. If you've got an old garden gnome that needs a retirement home, a nice place in the country, we'll take him free of charge. Fishing. Lovely views."

Within days we had fifty old gnomes. Within weeks we had a hundred. One by one we repaired them and painted them. We put them out in the fields, under the trees, all over the place, and the ones with the fishing rods we put down by the stream. When we were ready we put up the sign outside: "Mister Skip's Pixie Park". We charged one euro to get in and they came in their thousands. We gave all of them a pixie hat to put on, big and red and floppy, to make them feel at home, and then they went on a tour of "Mister Skip's Pixie Park."

As for Mister Skip, he stays by the front door looking out over his park, and he isn't lonely any more. He talks to me all the time now, you can hardly stop him. He's so happy.

Yesterday evening I was sitting out there with him after all the visitors had gone, just watching the sun go down over the hill.

"Aren't we the lucky ones, Mister Skip?" I said.

"Luck?" replied Mister Skip. "What's luck got to do with it?" And when he began to chuckle, it echoed from hill to hill and down the valley, so that it seemed as if every gnome and pixie in the park was chuckling with him. Perhaps they were.

Witch-in-Training
Flying Lessons

Maeve Friel

Illustrated by Nathan Reed

On Jessica's tenth birthday she discovers that she is a witch! With Miss Strega as her teacher, and a broomstick to fly, Jessica is ready to begin her training. The first book in a magical new series.

ISBN 0 00 713341 3

An imprint of HarperCollins*Publishers*

www.roaringgoodreads.co.uk

Daisy May

Jean Ure

Illustrated by Karen Donnelly

For the first ten years of her life, Daisy lives in the Foundling Hospital with lots of other orphans. But on her tenth birthday she goes to work at the Dobell Academy for young ladies. There she watches, listens, learns and dreams. A 'rags-to-riches' story with a difference, where dreams really can come true!

ISBN 0 00 713369 3

An imprint of HarperCollins*Publishers*

www.roaringgoodreads.co.uk

Order Form

To order direct from the publishers, just make a list of the titles you want and fill in the form below:

Name ....

Address ....

....

....

Send to: Dept 6, HarperCollins Publishers Ltd, Westerhill Road, Bishopbriggs, Glasgow G64 2QT.

Please enclose a cheque or postal order to the value of the cover price, plus:

e first book, and 25p per rdered.

ervice charge. Books will es for airmail despatch

ervice is available to mex or Switch cards

rCollins*Publishers*